Time's Ripple

Mrigendra Bharti

Published by Sellbrochure Vymish Entertainment, 2024.

Table of Contents

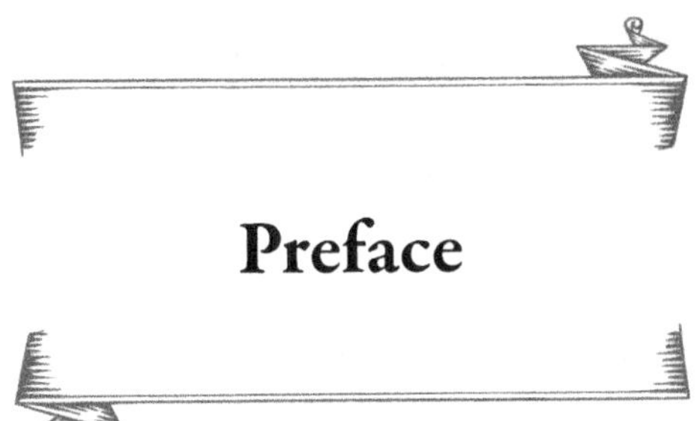

Preface

"Time's Ripple" is a tale that delves into the intricate and often unpredictable dance of time and its profound effects on our lives. At the heart of this narrative is Aditya, a brilliant physicist whose discovery of an ancient artifact grants him the extraordinary ability to traverse the temporal landscape. His journey is one of ambition and introspection, as he grapples with the ethical implications and unforeseen consequences of his actions across time.

The inspiration for this story comes from a deep fascination with the concept of time travel and the butterfly effect—the idea that small actions can have vast and sometimes unintended repercussions. As humans, we often ponder the "what ifs" of our past, wondering how different choices might have led us down alternate paths. "Time's Ripple" explores these themes, presenting a narrative that is both a cautionary tale and a philosophical exploration of fate, free will, and the interconnectedness of events.

Throughout Aditya's journey, we witness the delicate balance of time and the chaos that ensues when one attempts to alter its course. His story serves as a reminder of the inherent complexity of our existence and the importance of accepting the flow of time. As readers, we are invited to reflect on our own lives and the seemingly insignificant moments that have shaped our destinies.

I hope that "Time's Ripple" captivates your imagination and provides a thought-provoking exploration of the mysteries of time. May it inspire you to consider the ripples of your own actions and the timeless echoes they create in the fabric of reality.

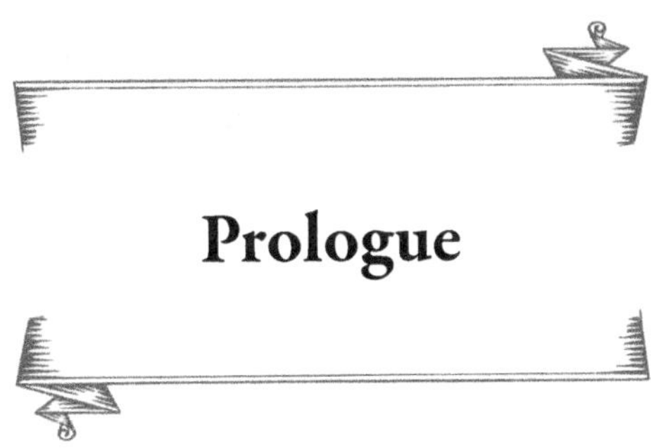

Prologue

The winds whispered secrets as they swept through the ancient Himalayan valley, carrying tales of forgotten times. Amidst the towering peaks and serene silence, an enigma lay buried, waiting for centuries to be uncovered. The temple, hidden away from the prying eyes of the modern world, held within its stone walls a relic of unimaginable power—an artifact that could alter the very fabric of time.

Aditya stood at the entrance of the temple, his heart pounding with a mixture of excitement and trepidation. As a physicist, he had always been drawn to the mysteries of the universe, but this was beyond anything he had ever imagined. The amulet, its surface etched with cryptic symbols, seemed to pulse with a life of its own. The moment his fingers brushed against it, a cascade of memories and possibilities flooded his mind.

In an instant, he was transported to his childhood home, the familiar scent of his mother's cooking wafting through the air. The realization hit him—this was no ordinary artifact. It was a key to the past, a bridge to the future, a doorway to infinite possibilities.

With great power comes great responsibility, he reminded himself, but the temptation was too strong. The chance to right wrongs, to fix mistakes, to create a better world was irresistible.

Little did Aditya know, his journey would lead him down a path fraught with paradoxes and dilemmas, where every action would send ripples through time, altering the course of history in ways he could never predict.

As he clutched the amulet, he made a silent vow—to use its power wisely. But time, as he would soon learn, is a force beyond control, and its ripples can become waves, sweeping away all certainty in their wake.

Thus began Aditya's odyssey through the tapestry of time, a journey that would challenge his understanding of reality, test his resolve, and ultimately, teach him the profound truth about the delicate balance of existence.

Acknowledgment

Writing "Time's Ripple" has been an extraordinary journey, and I am deeply grateful for the support and inspiration that have made this book possible.

I would like to express my heartfelt appreciation to my friends and family, whose encouragement and belief in me have been unwavering. Your patience and understanding have been invaluable throughout this process.

To the many individuals whose insights and conversations have sparked ideas and deepened my understanding of time and its complexities, thank you for sharing your knowledge and perspectives.

Lastly, to the readers who have embarked on this journey with me, your curiosity and imagination are the true driving forces behind this story. I hope "Time's Ripple" resonates with you and leaves you contemplating the fascinating dance of time and fate.

Thank you all for being a part of this adventure.

Introduction

Time has always been a subject of endless fascination and speculation. From ancient myths to modern science fiction, the concept of traveling through time, altering past events, and witnessing future possibilities has captivated human imagination. The allure lies in the tantalizing "what ifs"—the chance to change the course of one's life, to correct mistakes, or to foresee and prevent disasters.

"Time's Ripple" is a story that ventures into this realm of infinite possibilities. It follows Aditya, a brilliant physicist whose encounter with an ancient artifact grants him the power to traverse the temporal landscape. Through his journey, we explore the profound implications of his actions, each decision sending ripples across the continuum of time.

This book is not just about the mechanics of time travel, but also a deep dive into the ethical and philosophical questions it raises. What happens when we tamper with the past? Can we really shape the future to our liking, or are we merely pawns in a grand, predetermined scheme? How do the smallest actions reverberate through time, creating waves that shape the destinies of individuals and civilizations?

Aditya's story is one of discovery and caution. It is a narrative that intertwines scientific curiosity with human emotions, showcasing the intricate balance between ambition and humility. As he navigates the complexities of time, Aditya learns that with great power comes not just great responsibility, but also an understanding of the limits of control and the acceptance of life's inherent uncertainties.

"Time's Ripple" invites readers to join Aditya on his extraordinary adventure, to ponder the delicate interplay of cause and effect, and to reflect on their own lives and the ripples they create. Through this journey, may you find not only entertainment but also a deeper appreciation for the mysteries of time and existence.

Welcome to the world of "Time's Ripple." Prepare to be transported across the tapestry of time, where every moment is interconnected, and every action has the potential to reshape reality.

Connect With Mrigendra,
Thank you very much for choosing this book.
You can also connect with me on Instagram,
https://www.instagram.com/i_mrigendrabharti.official
With Love,
Mrigendra Bharti

Chapter 1: The Discovery

The Expedition

The crisp mountain air cut through Aditya's lungs as he trudged up the rugged terrain of the Himalayan foothills. His backpack weighed heavy on his shoulders, filled with supplies for the expedition ahead. Beside him, his team members marched in unison, their excitement palpable in the air.

The sun was just beginning to rise, casting a warm glow over the snow-capped peaks in the distance. Aditya couldn't help but feel a sense of awe and reverence for the natural beauty that surrounded him. This was his element—the great outdoors, where mysteries waited to be uncovered, and discoveries lay hidden beneath the earth's surface.

As they reached the crest of a hill, Aditya's heart skipped a beat at the sight before him. Spread out below was a vast expanse of untouched wilderness, dotted with lush greenery and meandering streams. Nestled within this pristine landscape was their destination—a remote valley rumored to hold the secrets of an ancient civilization.

The journey had been long and arduous, but Aditya knew it would all be worth it. For years, he had been fascinated by the myths and legends surrounding the Himalayas—the tales of lost cities, buried treasures, and mystical artifacts waiting to be unearthed. Now, finally, he had the chance to see if there was any truth to these stories.

Leading the expedition was Dr. Gupta, a renowned archaeologist with a passion for uncovering the mysteries of the past. His weathered face bore the marks of countless expeditions, his eyes alive with the thrill of discovery. Aditya had always admired Dr. Gupta's dedication and expertise, and he felt honored to be part of his team.

As they descended into the valley below, Aditya's anticipation grew with each step. He couldn't shake the feeling that they were on the brink of something extraordinary—a once-in-a-lifetime opportunity to make history. His mind raced with possibilities, imagining the artifacts they might find, the secrets they might uncover.

Hours passed as they trekked deeper into the valley, the landscape shifting around them. Tall trees gave way to rocky cliffs, and the air grew thick with the scent of ancient earth. Aditya felt a sense of reverence wash over him, as if he were treading on sacred ground.

Finally, they reached their destination—a clearing nestled at the base of a towering cliff. Before them stood the entrance to a cave, its mouth shrouded in darkness. Aditya's heart pounded with excitement as Dr. Gupta motioned for the team to gather round.

"We have arrived," Dr. Gupta announced, his voice echoing off the walls of the cave. "This is where our journey begins."

Aditya felt a surge of adrenaline as he stepped into the cave, his senses tingling with anticipation. The air was cool and musty, filled with the scent of damp earth. As they ventured deeper into the darkness, Aditya couldn't shake the feeling that they were being watched—that ancient eyes were upon them, waiting to reveal their secrets.

And then, as if in response to his thoughts, a glimmer of light caught his eye. Aditya's heart skipped a beat as he followed the source of the light, his breath catching in his throat. There, nestled among the rocks, was a small, glowing object—a relic from a bygone era, waiting to be discovered.

Without hesitation, Aditya reached out and grasped the object in his hand, his fingers trembling with excitement. As he held it aloft, the object pulsed with a strange energy, filling the cave with an ethereal glow.

"What is it?" one of his teammates asked, their voice barely a whisper.

Aditya smiled, his mind racing with possibilities. "I believe," he said, his voice filled with wonder, "that we have just uncovered the key to unlocking the mysteries of time itself."

The First Leap

Aditya's fingers trembled as he held the glowing object, his mind racing with the possibilities of what it could be. The artifact seemed to pulse with an otherworldly energy, casting a soft glow that illuminated the dark recesses of the cave. It was unlike anything he had ever seen before—a relic from a time long forgotten, waiting to reveal its secrets.

As Aditya examined the artifact more closely, he noticed intricate symbols etched into its surface. They seemed to dance and shift in the dim light, their meaning elusive yet tantalizing. He felt a surge of excitement coursing through his veins—a feeling of destiny unfolding before him.

"Dr. Gupta, look at this!" Aditya called out, his voice echoing off the cavern walls. "I think we've found something incredible!"

Dr. Gupta hurried over, his eyes widening in amazement as he caught sight of the artifact. "By the gods," he exclaimed, his voice filled with awe. "This could be the discovery of a lifetime."

The rest of the team gathered around, their faces alight with curiosity and excitement. They crowded in, eager to catch a glimpse of the mysterious object that Aditya held in his hands.

"What do you think it is?" one of the team members asked, his voice hushed with reverence.

Aditya hesitated, his mind racing as he searched for an answer. "I'm not sure," he admitted, his voice barely above a whisper. "But I believe it may hold the key to unlocking the secrets of time itself."

The words hung in the air, sending a shiver down Aditya's spine. He could feel the weight of their significance—the realization that they were on the brink of something monumental. The artifact held the promise of answers to questions that had plagued humanity for centuries—the nature of time, the mysteries of the universe, the very essence of existence.

Without hesitation, Aditya made a decision. Gripping the artifact tightly in his hand, he closed his eyes and focused his thoughts, willing himself to unlock its power. In an instant, he felt a surge of energy coursing through him, lifting him from the ground and carrying him through the fabric of time itself.

When Aditya opened his eyes, he found himself standing in a place he knew all too well—his childhood home. The familiar sights and sounds washed over him, filling him with a sense of nostalgia and longing. He could hear his mother's laughter echoing through the halls, see the sunlight streaming through the windows, feel the warmth of his father's embrace.

But something was different. Something had changed.

As Aditya looked around, he realized with a start that he was not alone. Standing before him was a figure from his past—a childhood friend whom he had not seen in years. The friend looked at him with a mixture of confusion and disbelief, as if unsure of what to make of Aditya's sudden appearance.

"Aditya?" the friend asked, his voice tinged with uncertainty. "Is that really you?"

Aditya felt a lump forming in his throat as he nodded, his heart pounding with emotion. "Yes," he replied, his voice barely above a whisper. "It's me."

And in that moment, as Aditya stood face to face with his past, he realized that nothing would ever be the same again. He had taken the first leap into the unknown, and there was no turning back.

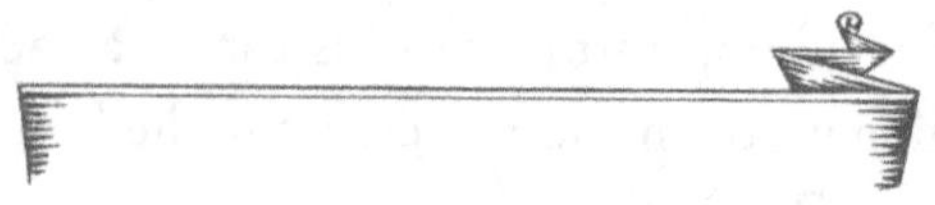

The Ripple Effect Begins

Aditya's heart raced as he stood face to face with his childhood friend, the implications of his sudden appearance sinking in. He had taken the first leap into the unknown, and now he had to navigate the repercussions of his actions. The artifact in his hand pulsed with a faint glow, a silent reminder of the power he now wielded.

"Aditya, what's going on?" his friend asked, his eyes wide with confusion. "How did you get here?"

Aditya struggled to find the right words, his mind racing as he tried to come to terms with the situation. "I...I'm not sure," he admitted, his voice trembling with uncertainty. "It's...complicated."

His friend frowned, clearly unconvinced by Aditya's vague explanation. "Complicated how?" he pressed, his curiosity piqued.

Aditya hesitated, unsure of how much to reveal. He knew that he couldn't divulge the truth about the artifact—that it held the power to manipulate time itself. It was a secret that he had to keep, lest it fall into the wrong hands.

"I...I don't know how to explain it," Aditya stammered, his mind racing for a plausible explanation. "It's...like...I just...appeared here, out of nowhere."

His friend regarded him with a skeptical expression, clearly not convinced by Aditya's explanation. "That's...weird," he remarked, his tone tinged with uncertainty. "But I guess stranger things have happened."

Aditya breathed a sigh of relief, grateful that his friend seemed willing to accept his story, at least for the time being. But deep down, he knew that he couldn't keep the truth hidden forever. Sooner or later, he would have to confront the reality of his newfound abilities—and the consequences that came with them.

As Aditya and his friend caught up on old times, Aditya couldn't shake the feeling of unease that gnawed at him. He knew that he had to be careful, that every action he took had the potential to alter the course of history in ways he couldn't predict. The responsibility weighed heavily on his shoulders, a constant reminder of the power he now held.

But despite the uncertainty of the future, Aditya couldn't help but feel a sense of excitement at the possibilities that lay ahead. With the artifact in his possession, he had the power to shape his own destiny—to right wrongs, to fix mistakes, to create a better world. It was a daunting task, to be sure, but one that he was determined to undertake.

As the day drew to a close and Aditya bid his friend farewell, he knew that his journey was only just beginning. The artifact pulsed in his hand, its glow casting long shadows on the ground. And as Aditya looked up at the stars twinkling in the night sky, he couldn't help but wonder what other secrets lay waiting to be uncovered in the vast expanse of time.

Temptation and Resolve

As Aditya made his way back to the archaeological camp, his mind buzzed with a whirlwind of thoughts and emotions. The encounter with his childhood friend had only scratched the surface of the potential consequences of his newfound abilities. He knew that he had to tread carefully, but the allure of the artifact's power was undeniable.

As he approached the campsite, Aditya found himself lost in thought, oblivious to the hustle and bustle around him. Dr. Gupta greeted him with a warm smile, but Aditya could sense the tension in the air—the anticipation of what lay ahead.

"Aditya, you look like you've seen a ghost," Dr. Gupta remarked, his brow furrowed with concern. "Is everything alright?"

Aditya forced a smile, masking the turmoil brewing beneath the surface. "I'm fine, Dr. Gupta," he replied, his voice steady despite the turmoil within. "Just...a lot on my mind, I suppose."

Dr. Gupta regarded him with a knowing look, as if sensing the weight of Aditya's unspoken thoughts. "Well, you're not alone, my boy," he said, clapping Aditya on the shoulder. "We're all in this together."

Aditya nodded, grateful for Dr. Gupta's reassurance. But deep down, he knew that he was on his own—that the decisions he made in the days to come would shape the course of his own destiny.

As night fell and the camp settled into an uneasy silence, Aditya found himself drawn to the artifact once again. It lay nestled in his pack, its glow a silent reminder of the power it held. He knew that he had to be careful, that every action he took had the potential to alter the course of history in ways he couldn't predict.

But the temptation was too strong to resist. With a trembling hand, Aditya withdrew the artifact from his pack, its surface shimmering in the moonlight. He felt a surge of adrenaline coursing through his veins—a sense of exhilaration at the possibilities that lay before him.

And so, with a mixture of trepidation and excitement, Aditya made a decision. Gripping the artifact tightly in his hand, he closed his eyes and focused his thoughts, willing himself to unlock its power once again. In an instant, he felt a surge of energy coursing through him, lifting him from the ground and carrying him through the fabric of time itself.

As he vanished into the darkness, Aditya knew that he was embarking on a journey from which there would be no turning back. The artifact pulsed with a faint glow, casting long shadows on the ground—a silent witness to the choices that would shape the destiny of all who dared to wield its power.

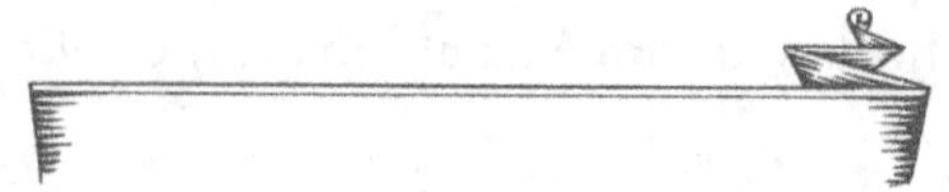

Chapter 2: The First Changes

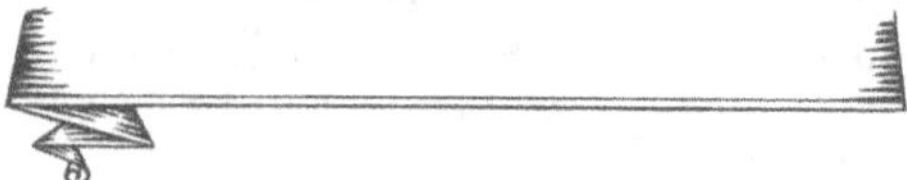

Saving His Parents

Aditya emerged from the temporal vortex, his senses reeling as he adjusted to his surroundings. He found himself standing in the familiar surroundings of his childhood home, but something was different. The air crackled with an electric energy, and Aditya could sense the weight of his mission pressing down on him.

Taking a deep breath to steady his nerves, Aditya glanced around, his eyes scanning the familiar surroundings for any signs of his parents. It didn't take long for him to spot them—they were in the kitchen, his mother bustling about as she prepared dinner, his father seated at the table, lost in thought.

With a sense of determination coursing through him, Aditya made his way towards them, his heart pounding in his chest. He knew what he had to do—he had to save them, to prevent the tragic accident that had taken their lives far too soon.

"Mom, Dad," Aditya called out, his voice trembling with emotion as he approached them. "I need to talk to you."

His parents turned to him, their faces registering a mixture of surprise and concern. "Aditya, what are you doing here?" his mother asked, her brow furrowed with confusion.

Aditya took a deep breath, steeling himself for what he was about to do. "I...I know this is going to sound crazy," he began, his voice faltering slightly. "But I'm from the future. And I'm here to save you."

His parents exchanged a puzzled glance, clearly unsure of what to make of Aditya's declaration. "Save us from what?" his father asked, his voice tinged with skepticism.

Aditya hesitated, knowing that he couldn't reveal too much without altering the course of history. "From...from a terrible accident," he replied, choosing his words carefully. "But if you listen to me and follow my instructions, I can prevent it from happening."

His parents regarded him with a mixture of disbelief and concern, but Aditya could see the glimmer of hope in their eyes. He knew that he had to act fast, before they had a chance to question him further.

"Come with me," Aditya said, gesturing towards the door. "There's not much time."

With a sense of urgency, Aditya led his parents out of the house, his mind racing with the details of the plan he had formulated. He knew that he had to be careful, that even the slightest deviation from the timeline could have disastrous consequences.

As they reached the spot where the accident was supposed to occur, Aditya felt a surge of adrenaline coursing through him. This was it—the moment of truth, the chance to change the course of his own history.

With a steady hand, Aditya guided his parents to safety, ensuring that they were out of harm's way. And then, with a sense of relief washing over him, he watched as the accident that had claimed their lives unfolded before his eyes.

But as the dust settled and the danger passed, Aditya realized with a sinking feeling in the pit of his stomach that something was wrong. The timeline had shifted, but not in the way he had anticipated. And as he looked around at the altered landscape before him, he knew that he had unleashed forces beyond his control.

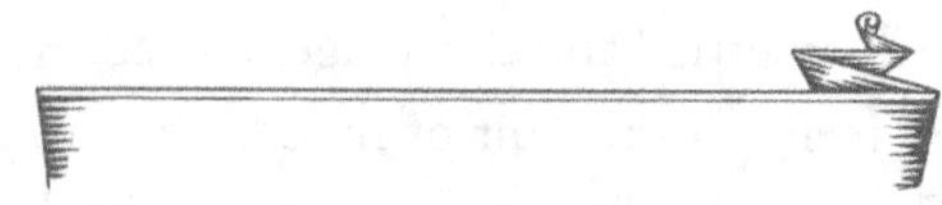

Unintended Consequences

The aftermath of Aditya's intervention left him reeling, grappling with the unintended consequences of his actions. While he had succeeded in preventing the accident that claimed his parents' lives, the ripple effects of his interference began to reveal themselves in unexpected ways.

As Aditya surveyed the altered timeline, he noticed subtle shifts in the world around him. Familiar landmarks appeared slightly different, and the atmosphere felt charged with an unfamiliar energy. It was as if reality itself was struggling to adjust to the changes he had wrought.

But the true extent of the consequences became apparent when Aditya returned home to find that his parents were not the only ones affected by his intervention. Friends, neighbors, and even acquaintances had undergone significant changes, their lives reshaped by the absence of the tragedy that had defined their existence.

Aditya's childhood friend, whom he had saved from the accident, had taken a different path in life, pursuing a career that he had never considered before. His neighbor, who had once been a close family friend, now regarded him with suspicion and distrust, as if sensing the disruption in the fabric of reality.

But perhaps the most jarring revelation came when Aditya discovered that his own life had been altered in ways he could never have imagined. Relationships that had once been stable and secure now seemed strained and uncertain, as if the foundation upon which they were built had been shaken to its core.

As Aditya grappled with the consequences of his actions, he couldn't help but feel a sense of guilt and regret weighing heavily on his shoulders. He had set out to change the past, to rewrite history in his favor, but in doing so, he had inadvertently unleashed a chain of events that threatened to unravel the very fabric of time itself.

But amidst the chaos and uncertainty, Aditya found a glimmer of hope—a determination to set things right, to undo the damage he had caused. With renewed resolve, he set out to confront the challenges that lay ahead, knowing that the fate of both his past and future hung in the balance.

And as he embarked on his journey, Aditya couldn't help but wonder what other unintended consequences awaited him, lurking just beyond the horizon. But one thing was certain—he would face them head-on, armed with the knowledge that even the smallest actions could have far-reaching implications in the ever-shifting tapestry of time.

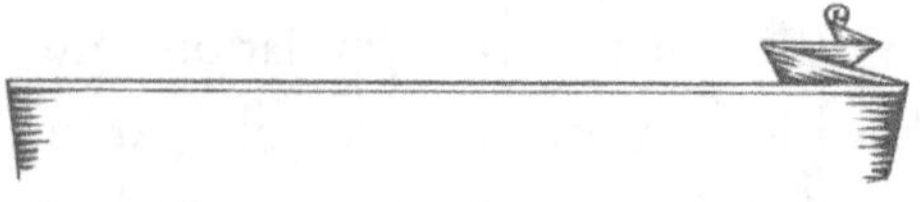

Technological Leap

As Aditya grappled with the repercussions of altering the past, he couldn't shake the feeling of unease that gnawed at him. The changes he had wrought had reshaped the world in unexpected ways, and he could sense the fragile balance of reality teetering on the edge of chaos.

But amidst the uncertainty, Aditya found himself drawn to the allure of the artifact's power once again. With each passing day, its pull grew stronger, tempting him with the promise of even greater changes. And so, with a sense of trepidation and excitement, Aditya made a decision—to use the artifact to usher in a new era of technological advancement.

With a determined stride, Aditya set out to implement his plan, drawing on his knowledge of future innovations to introduce groundbreaking technology to the world ahead of its time. From renewable energy sources to advanced medical treatments, Aditya spared no expense in his quest to reshape the future in his image.

But as the days turned into weeks and the weeks into months, Aditya began to realize the unintended consequences of his actions. While his innovations brought about unprecedented progress and prosperity, they also unleashed a wave of societal upheaval and ethical dilemmas.

The rapid pace of technological advancement left many struggling to keep up, their livelihoods threatened by obsolescence and automation. And as the gap between the haves and have-nots widened, tensions simmered beneath the surface, threatening to erupt into open conflict.

But perhaps the most troubling consequence of Aditya's actions was the erosion of human connection and empathy in the face of relentless progress. As society became increasingly reliant on technology, people grew more isolated and disconnected from one another, their humanity slowly fading away.

As Aditya grappled with the consequences of his actions, he couldn't help but feel a sense of remorse for the role he had played in shaping the world's future. But despite the challenges that lay ahead, he remained determined to set things right, to undo the damage he had caused and restore balance to the timeline.

And so, with a heavy heart and a renewed sense of purpose, Aditya set out on a new journey—one that would test his resolve and push him to the limits of his abilities. For he knew that the fate of the world—and his own destiny—hung in the balance, and that only by confronting the consequences of his actions head-on could he hope to find redemption.

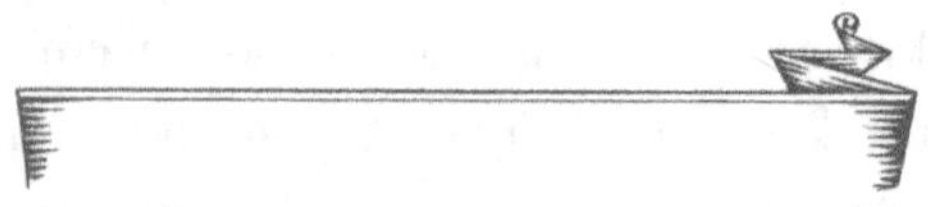

Encounter with Future Self

As Aditya grappled with the unintended consequences of his actions, he found himself confronted with a visitor from a future he could scarcely comprehend—himself. The encounter shook him to his core, forcing him to confront the full extent of the havoc he had wrought upon the fabric of time.

The future version of Aditya stood before him, a mirror image of himself yet with eyes that bore the weight of countless lifetimes. There was a gravity to his presence, a sense of wisdom and experience that Aditya couldn't help but envy.

"Who are you?" Aditya asked, his voice trembling with uncertainty.

"I am you," his future self replied, his tone somber. "Or rather, I am what you will become if you continue down this path."

Aditya felt a chill run down his spine at the implications of his future self's words. He knew that he had to listen, to heed the warnings of the man standing before him, if he hoped to have any chance of setting things right.

"I've seen what happens if you continue to meddle with time," his future self continued, his voice tinged with regret. "The consequences are far greater than you can imagine."

Aditya felt a knot forming in his stomach as he listened to his future self's dire warnings. He knew that he had to act, to find a way to undo the damage he had caused before it was too late.

"But how?" Aditya asked, his voice filled with desperation. "How can I fix this?"

His future self regarded him with a solemn expression, as if weighing his words carefully. "You must let go of the past," he replied, his voice firm. "You must accept that some things are beyond your control, and focus on the present."

Aditya nodded, a sense of determination welling up within him. He knew that his future self was right—that he had to let go of his obsession with changing the past and focus on making things right in the here and now.

Armed with a newfound sense of purpose, Aditya set out to confront the challenges that lay ahead, knowing that the fate of the world—and his own destiny—hung in the balance. For he knew that only by confronting the consequences of his actions head-on could he hope to find redemption and set things right once and for all.

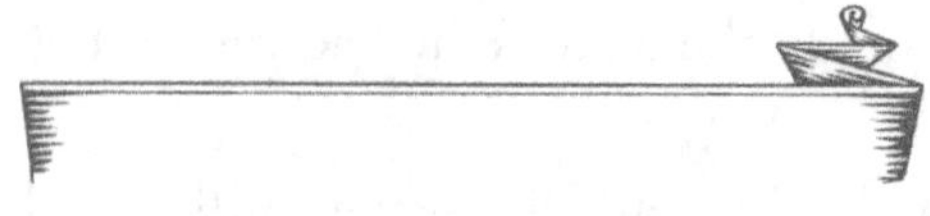

Averting a War

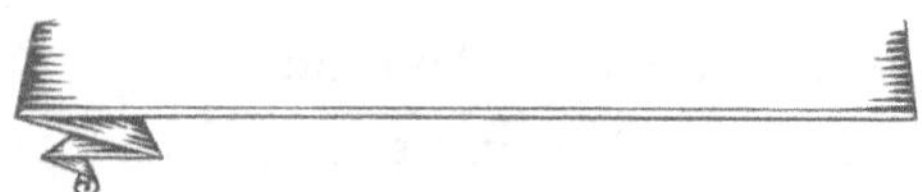

Aditya's resolve to set things right propelled him forward into a new mission: to prevent a major historical conflict that had plagued humanity for centuries. Armed with the knowledge of past events and the power of the artifact, he embarked on a journey through time to alter the course of history.

His destination was a pivotal moment in the annals of human conflict—a meeting of world leaders on the brink of war. As Aditya materialized in the midst of the tense negotiations, he felt the weight of history bearing down on him. The fate of millions hung in the balance, and it was up to him to tip the scales in favor of peace.

With a steady hand and a calm demeanor, Aditya approached the leaders gathered before him, his mind racing with strategies to avert the impending conflict. He knew that he had to tread carefully, to navigate the delicate intricacies of diplomacy and power politics with finesse.

As the negotiations unfolded, Aditya found himself drawing on his knowledge of future events to sway the outcome in favor of peace. He employed a combination of persuasion, compromise, and even subtle manipulation to steer the conversation away from the brink of war.

But despite his best efforts, Aditya soon realized that altering the course of history was no easy task. The leaders were entrenched in their positions, their egos and ambitions standing in the way of progress. And as tensions flared and tempers flared, Aditya feared that his mission might be doomed to failure.

But just when all seemed lost, a breakthrough occurred—a moment of clarity that shattered the barriers of mistrust and suspicion that had divided the leaders for so long. Through a combination of skillful negotiation and timely intervention, Aditya managed to broker a historic peace agreement, averting the war that had threatened to engulf the world in chaos.

As the leaders signed the peace treaty and embraced one another in a show of solidarity, Aditya felt a surge of relief wash over him. He had succeeded in his mission, altering the course of history in a way that would shape the destiny of generations to come.

But even as he celebrated his victory, Aditya knew that the consequences of his actions would ripple far beyond the confines of the present. The world had been forever changed by his intervention, and only time would tell what new challenges and conflicts lay ahead in the ever-unfolding tapestry of human history.

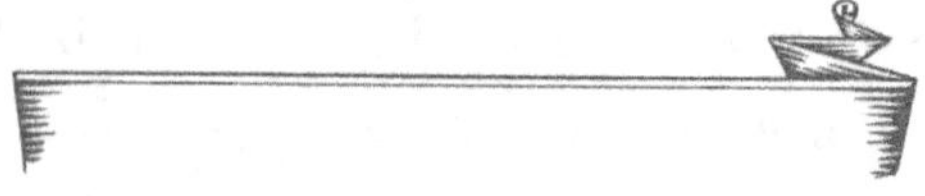

The Butterfly Effect

Aditya's success in averting the war brought temporary relief, but it also unleashed a torrent of unintended consequences that threatened to unravel the fabric of reality itself. As he returned to the present, he found the world changed in ways he could never have imagined.

The peace treaty he had brokered had set off a chain reaction of events, reshaping the geopolitical landscape and altering the course of history in unforeseen ways. Borders shifted, alliances formed and dissolved, and old rivalries reignited with newfound intensity.

But perhaps the most alarming consequence of Aditya's actions was the emergence of a new threat—a shadowy organization hell-bent on exploiting the chaos for their own sinister purposes. Led by a charismatic yet enigmatic leader, they operated in the shadows, pulling the strings of power with ruthless efficiency.

As Aditya delved deeper into the mystery of the organization, he uncovered a web of intrigue and deceit that stretched back centuries. They had infiltrated every level of society, manipulating events from behind the scenes to further their own agenda of domination and control.

But as Aditya soon discovered, the organization's ambitions extended far beyond mere political power. They sought to harness the power of the artifact for their own nefarious purposes, using it to rewrite history in their image and reshape the world according to their whims.

Determined to stop them at all costs, Aditya embarked on a dangerous game of cat and mouse, racing against time to uncover their true motives and thwart their plans. With each revelation, he found himself drawn deeper into the heart of darkness, confronting enemies both old and new in a desperate bid to save humanity from destruction.

But as the stakes grew higher and the danger more imminent, Aditya realized that he couldn't do it alone. He needed allies—trusted friends and colleagues who shared his vision of a better world, free from the shackles of tyranny and oppression.

And so, with a sense of determination burning in his heart, Aditya set out to gather a team of like-minded individuals, each with their own unique skills and abilities. Together, they would stand against the forces of darkness and fight for the future of humanity, no matter the cost.

But as they prepared to confront the organization head-on, Aditya couldn't shake the feeling of unease that gnawed at him. The consequences of his actions had set off a chain reaction that threatened to engulf the world in chaos, and only by confronting the darkness within could he hope to bring about the dawn of a new era of peace and prosperity.

The Alliance Formed

As Aditya and his newly formed team delved deeper into the mystery of the shadowy organization, they encountered numerous obstacles and challenges along the way. But with each setback, they grew stronger and more determined to uncover the truth and put an end to the organization's nefarious plans.

Their investigations led them to dark alleys and hidden corners of the world, where danger lurked at every turn. They encountered spies, mercenaries, and double agents, each more cunning and ruthless than the last. But Aditya and his team refused to be deterred, pressing forward with unwavering resolve.

Along the way, they forged unlikely alliances with individuals from all walks of life—renegade scientists, rogue hackers, and even disillusioned members of the organization itself. Together, they pooled their resources and expertise, forming a formidable force against the dark forces that threatened to engulf the world.

But perhaps the most surprising ally of all was Aditya's future self, who appeared sporadically to offer guidance and assistance in their quest. Though their encounters were brief and cryptic, they provided valuable insights and glimpses into the future that helped Aditya and his team stay one step ahead of their adversaries.

As they pieced together the puzzle of the organization's true motives, Aditya and his team uncovered a shocking revelation—the artifact held the key to unlocking untold power, power that could reshape the very fabric of reality itself. And the organization would stop at nothing to harness that power for their own sinister purposes.

Armed with this knowledge, Aditya and his team redoubled their efforts, racing against time to prevent the organization from obtaining the artifact and unleashing untold chaos upon the world. They infiltrated secret bases, hacked into encrypted databases, and engaged in daring rescues and sabotage missions, all in the name of preserving the delicate balance of reality.

But as they closed in on their elusive adversaries, Aditya couldn't shake the feeling of unease that gnawed at him. The fate of the world hung in the balance, and the consequences of their actions would reverberate far beyond the confines of the present. But with their alliance forged in the crucible of adversity, Aditya and his team stood ready to confront whatever challenges lay ahead, united in their determination to save humanity from the brink of destruction.

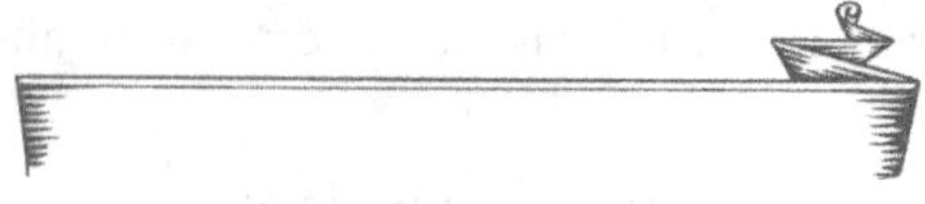

The Final Showdown

As Aditya and his team closed in on the shadowy organization, tension hung thick in the air like a storm on the horizon. They had faced countless obstacles and challenges along the way, but now they stood on the brink of the final showdown—a battle that would determine the fate of humanity itself.

Their journey had taken them to the farthest reaches of the globe, from the towering skyscrapers of urban metropolises to the desolate wilderness of remote jungles. They had encountered enemies both human and inhuman, each more formidable than the last. But through sheer determination and unwavering resolve, they had persevered.

Now, as they stood before the organization's stronghold, Aditya could feel the weight of destiny bearing down on him. The artifact pulsed with an otherworldly energy in his hand, a silent reminder of the power that lay within his grasp. But he knew that wielding such power came with a heavy price—a price that he was willing to pay to protect the world he loved.

With a silent nod to his team, Aditya led the charge into the heart of darkness, his heart pounding with adrenaline as they breached the organization's defenses. They fought with a ferocity born of desperation, each blow striking a blow against the forces of tyranny and oppression.

But as they pressed deeper into the stronghold, they encountered fierce resistance from the organization's elite soldiers and their leader, a shadowy figure shrouded in mystery and menace. The battle raged on, each side refusing to back down in the face of overwhelming odds.

In the midst of the chaos, Aditya found himself locked in a deadly duel with the organization's leader, their blades clashing in a symphony of steel. With each blow, Aditya felt the weight of his past and future bearing down on him, driving him to fight with a strength and determination he never knew he possessed.

But just when all seemed lost, a glimmer of hope appeared on the horizon—a sudden shift in the balance of power that turned the tide of battle in their favor. With renewed resolve, Aditya and his team fought with renewed vigor, their determination unshakeable in the face of overwhelming adversity.

And then, in a final, climactic showdown, Aditya emerged victorious, his blade striking true and vanquishing the organization's leader once and for all. As the dust settled and the echoes of battle faded into the night, Aditya stood triumphant, his heart filled with a sense of relief and gratitude.

But even as he celebrated their hard-fought victory, Aditya knew that the journey was far from over. The consequences of their actions would reverberate far beyond the confines of the present, shaping the destiny of humanity for generations to come. But with their alliance forged in the crucible of adversity, Aditya and his team stood ready to confront whatever challenges lay ahead, united in their determination to protect the world from the forces of darkness and usher in a new era of peace and prosperity.

Chapter 4: Reckoning

Consequences Unveiled

In the aftermath of the final showdown, Aditya and his team found themselves grappling with the far-reaching consequences of their actions. Though they had emerged victorious, the world they returned to was irrevocably changed, and the scars of their battle ran deep.

The defeat of the shadowy organization had brought temporary relief, but it also left a power vacuum in its wake—a void that threatened to plunge the world into even greater chaos and uncertainty. Without a common enemy to unite against, old rivalries and grievances resurfaced, threatening to tear society apart at the seams.

As Aditya surveyed the wreckage of the organization's stronghold, he couldn't help but feel a sense of unease gnawing at him. The artifact, once a source of hope and power, now seemed like a cursed relic, its true nature and purpose still shrouded in mystery.

But even as Aditya grappled with his doubts and uncertainties, a new threat emerged on the horizon—a force more insidious and malevolent than anything they had faced before. Dark whispers echoed through the shadows, hinting at a power beyond comprehension, a darkness that threatened to consume everything in its path.

Determined to confront the looming threat head-on, Aditya and his team embarked on a new mission—a journey into the heart of darkness to uncover the truth behind the whispers and put an end to the looming menace once and for all.

But as they delved deeper into the mysteries of the artifact and the forces that sought to control it, they soon realized that their journey would not be an easy one. They encountered ancient guardians and forgotten guardians, each more powerful and enigmatic than the last, testing their skills and resolve to the limit.

And as they ventured further into the unknown, Aditya couldn't shake the feeling that they were being watched—that unseen eyes followed their every move, waiting for the perfect moment to strike. But with the fate of the world hanging in the balance, Aditya and his team pressed on, determined to confront whatever dangers lay ahead and uncover the truth behind the artifact's true nature.

The Revelation

As Aditya and his team delved deeper into the heart of darkness, they uncovered long-forgotten truths that shook the very foundation of their reality. The artifact, they discovered, was not merely a tool of power—it was a key, a gateway to realms beyond comprehension, where ancient forces lay dormant, waiting to be unleashed.

With each revelation, Aditya felt the weight of the responsibility resting on his shoulders grow heavier. The fate of the world hung in the balance, and the consequences of their actions would shape the destiny of humanity for generations to come.

But amidst the chaos and uncertainty, a glimmer of hope emerged—a chance to set things right, to restore balance to the universe and prevent the forces of darkness from consuming everything in their path.

Armed with newfound knowledge and resolve, Aditya and his team set out to confront the ancient guardians that stood between them and the truth. They faced trials and tribulations beyond imagination, testing their courage and determination to the limit.

But as they neared their goal, they encountered an unexpected obstacle—a rival faction hell-bent on seizing the artifact for their own nefarious purposes. Led by a charismatic yet enigmatic leader, they possessed knowledge and power far beyond anything Aditya had ever encountered.

In a desperate bid to prevent the rival faction from obtaining the artifact, Aditya and his team engaged in a fierce battle that shook the very foundations of reality. With each blow, they fought with a ferocity born of desperation, knowing that failure was not an option.

But just when all seemed lost, a glimmer of hope emerged—a revelation that would change everything. The artifact, they discovered, was not a weapon of destruction—it was a catalyst for transformation, a beacon of hope in a world consumed by darkness.

With this newfound understanding, Aditya and his team forged an unlikely alliance with their former adversaries, uniting against a common enemy in a final, climactic showdown that would determine the fate of the universe itself.

And as the dust settled and the echoes of battle faded into the night, Aditya stood triumphant, his heart filled with a sense of peace and fulfillment. The artifact, once a source of fear and uncertainty, now stood as a symbol of hope and renewal, a testament to the resilience of the human spirit in the face of adversity.

But even as Aditya celebrated their hard-fought victory, he knew that the journey was far from over. The forces of darkness would not rest until they had been vanquished once and for all, and only by standing together could humanity hope to overcome the challenges that lay ahead. And so, with a renewed sense of purpose and unity, Aditya and his team set out to confront whatever trials and tribulations awaited them in the ever-unfolding tapestry of time.

Redemption and Sacrifice

As Aditya and his team basked in the aftermath of their hard-fought victory, a sense of peace settled over the world—a fragile calm born from the ashes of chaos and destruction. The forces of darkness had been vanquished, their threat neutralized by the combined efforts of Aditya and his allies.

But amidst the celebration, a somber truth lingered in the air—the cost of victory had been high, and not all who had fought alongside them had lived to see the dawn of a new era. Brave souls had sacrificed everything in the name of freedom and justice, their memories etched forever in the annals of history.

As Aditya stood amidst the fallen, he couldn't help but feel a sense of guilt and remorse weighing heavily on his heart. The lives lost in the battle weighed heavily on his conscience, a constant reminder of the sacrifices made in the name of a brighter future.

But even as he mourned the loss of his comrades, Aditya knew that their sacrifices had not been in vain. Their courage and selflessness had paved the way for a world free from the tyranny of darkness, a world where hope and freedom reigned supreme.

And so, with a heavy heart and a renewed sense of purpose, Aditya vowed to honor the memory of those who had fallen by continuing the fight for justice and equality. He knew that the road ahead would be fraught with challenges and obstacles, but he was determined to face them head-on, armed with the knowledge that the sacrifices of the past had not been in vain.

As the sun dipped below the horizon, casting long shadows across the battlefield, Aditya stood tall, his resolve unshakeable in the face of adversity. For he knew that the true measure of a hero was not in the battles they won or the enemies they vanquished, but in the sacrifices they were willing to make for the greater good.

And as he gazed out at the world stretched out before him, Aditya knew that the journey was far from over. The forces of darkness may have been defeated, but new challenges awaited on the horizon, each more formidable than the last.

But with the memory of his fallen comrades as his guiding light, Aditya stepped forward into the unknown, ready to confront whatever trials and tribulations lay ahead. For he knew that as long as there were those willing to fight for what was right, the flame of hope would never be extinguished, and the forces of darkness would never prevail.

The Legacy

In the wake of the final battle, Aditya and his team worked tirelessly to rebuild what had been lost, to mend the wounds of war and usher in a new era of peace and prosperity. Their victory had come at a great cost, but it had also forged bonds of friendship and unity that would endure for generations to come.

As the world slowly healed from the scars of conflict, Aditya and his allies dedicated themselves to ensuring that the sacrifices of the past were never forgotten. Memorials were erected in honor of the fallen, their names etched in stone as a reminder of their bravery and selflessness.

But perhaps the greatest tribute to their legacy was the newfound sense of unity and solidarity that blossomed in the aftermath of the war. Nations that had once been bitter enemies set aside their differences in the name of peace, forging alliances and treaties that would lay the foundation for a brighter future.

And amidst the rebuilding efforts, Aditya continued his quest to unlock the mysteries of the artifact, using its power for the betterment of humanity rather than for personal gain. With each discovery, he gained new insights into the nature of reality itself, pushing the boundaries of knowledge and understanding to new heights.

But even as he delved deeper into the mysteries of the artifact, Aditya remained vigilant, knowing that its power was not to be taken lightly. He vowed to use it wisely and responsibly, to ensure that the mistakes of the past were not repeated and that the world remained safe from the forces of darkness.

As the years passed, Aditya watched with pride as the world flourished under the banner of peace and progress. The sacrifices of the past had not been in vain—they had paved the way for a brighter future, one where hope and compassion reigned supreme.

And though the challenges of the future were many, Aditya faced them with courage and determination, secure in the knowledge that as long as there were those willing to fight for what was right, the forces of darkness would never prevail, and the legacy of those who had come before would live on for eternity.

Chapter 5: Beyond the Horizon

A New Journey Begins

With the world at peace and the forces of darkness vanquished, Aditya found himself standing at a crossroads, unsure of what the future held in store. The battles of the past had shaped him in ways he could never have imagined, but now a new journey beckoned—one filled with promise and possibility.

As he stood atop a windswept cliff overlooking the vast expanse of the ocean, Aditya felt a sense of anticipation coursing through his veins. The horizon stretched out before him, an endless canvas waiting to be painted with the colors of adventure and discovery.

With a sense of determination burning in his heart, Aditya made a decision—to embark on a new journey, to explore the unknown depths of the world and uncover the secrets that lay hidden beneath the surface.

Gathering his belongings and bidding farewell to his friends and allies, Aditya set out on his new adventure with a spring in his step and a sense of excitement in his heart. The world was vast and full of wonders, and he was determined to experience it all.

His journey took him to far-flung corners of the globe, from the bustling streets of exotic cities to the remote wilderness of untouched landscapes. Along the way, he encountered a myriad of cultures and civilizations, each with its own unique customs and traditions.

But amidst the beauty and wonder of his travels, Aditya couldn't shake the feeling that something was missing—a sense of purpose that had driven him forward in the darkest of times. He longed for a new challenge, a quest worthy of his skills and abilities.

And then, as if in answer to his prayers, a call to adventure echoed across the windswept plains—a rumor of a long-lost civilization hidden deep within the heart of the jungle, its secrets waiting to be uncovered by those brave enough to seek them out.

With a sense of excitement coursing through his veins, Aditya set out to unravel the mystery of the lost civilization, knowing that his journey would be fraught with danger and peril. But he was undeterred, for he knew that true adventure awaited just beyond the horizon, and he was determined to seize it with both hands.

Into the Unknown

As Aditya delved deeper into the heart of the jungle, he could feel the weight of history bearing down on him. The air was thick with the scent of ancient mysteries and forgotten secrets, and he knew that he was on the verge of uncovering something truly extraordinary.

Guided by rumors and whispers from the local villagers, Aditya pressed forward, his senses alert for any sign of danger or discovery. The jungle teemed with life, its lush foliage concealing hidden dangers and untold treasures alike.

But as the days turned into weeks and the weeks into months, Aditya found himself facing challenges unlike any he had encountered before. The jungle was a merciless mistress, testing his skills and resolve at every turn with its treacherous terrain and hostile inhabitants.

But amidst the trials and tribulations of his journey, Aditya also found moments of awe and wonder—the beauty of a cascading waterfall, the serenity of a starlit night sky, the camaraderie of newfound friends and allies.

And then, just when all seemed lost, a breakthrough occurred—a clue that would lead Aditya to the heart of the lost civilization he sought. With renewed determination, he pressed forward, his heart filled with anticipation at the prospect of uncovering the secrets that lay hidden within.

But as he ventured deeper into the heart of the jungle, Aditya soon realized that he was not alone. Dark forces lurked in the shadows, watching his every move with malevolent intent. They would stop at nothing to prevent him from uncovering the truth, to keep the secrets of the lost civilization buried forever.

Undeterred by the threats that surrounded him, Aditya pressed on, his resolve unshakeable in the face of adversity. For he knew that true adventure lay just beyond the horizon, and he was determined to seize it with both hands, no matter the cost.

And so, with a sense of determination burning in his heart, Aditya set out to confront the challenges that lay ahead, knowing that the journey would be fraught with danger and peril. But he was undeterred, for he knew that true greatness awaited just beyond the next bend in the road, and he was determined to reach out and seize it with both hands.

The Forgotten Temple

As Aditya ventured deeper into the heart of the jungle, the clues leading to the lost civilization grew stronger, guiding him towards his ultimate destination. Each step forward brought him closer to uncovering the mysteries that lay hidden within the dense foliage.

After weeks of arduous travel, Aditya stumbled upon the entrance to a forgotten temple, hidden beneath a thick canopy of trees. The air hummed with a palpable sense of ancient power, and Aditya knew that he had finally reached his destination.

With a sense of trepidation and excitement, Aditya stepped through the crumbling archway, his heart pounding with anticipation at the wonders that lay within. The temple was a labyrinth of twisting corridors and crumbling chambers, its walls adorned with faded hieroglyphs and intricate carvings.

As he explored the depths of the temple, Aditya uncovered secrets long thought lost to the sands of time—ancient artifacts and relics of a civilization that had vanished centuries ago. Each discovery filled him with a sense of wonder and awe, driving him forward in his quest for knowledge and understanding.

But amidst the treasures of the past, Aditya also encountered dangers that threatened to halt his progress at every turn. Booby traps and pitfalls lay in wait around every corner, testing his wits and reflexes as he navigated the treacherous passages of the temple.

But Aditya refused to be deterred, pressing forward with unwavering determination in the face of adversity. For he knew that the secrets of the lost civilization held the key to unlocking untold power and wisdom, and he was determined to uncover them at any cost.

And then, just when all seemed lost, Aditya stumbled upon a chamber unlike any he had encountered before—a chamber that held the key to unlocking the true nature of the artifact and the forces that had shaped his destiny.

With a sense of reverence, Aditya approached the ancient pedestal at the center of the chamber, its surface glowing with an otherworldly light. As he reached out to touch it, he felt a surge of energy course through his veins, filling him with a sense of purpose and clarity unlike anything he had ever experienced before.

And in that moment, as the secrets of the lost civilization were laid bare before him, Aditya knew that his journey was far from over. For the true adventure had only just begun, and he was ready to embrace it with open arms, knowing that whatever challenges lay ahead, he would face them with courage and determination, secure in the knowledge that he had the power to shape his own destiny.

The Final Revelation

As Aditya delved deeper into the heart of the ancient temple, he felt the weight of centuries pressing down on him, the echoes of the past whispering secrets long forgotten. Each step forward brought him closer to the ultimate truth—a truth that would shape the course of his destiny and the fate of the world.

In the innermost chamber of the temple, Aditya discovered a relic of unimaginable power—a crystal orb pulsating with an otherworldly energy. As he reached out to touch it, he felt a surge of power course through his veins, filling him with a sense of purpose and clarity.

With a sense of reverence, Aditya gazed into the depths of the orb, and in that moment, he saw the true nature of the artifact and the forces that had shaped his destiny. He saw visions of worlds beyond imagination, of civilizations rising and falling like waves upon the shore.

But amidst the chaos and turmoil of the vision, Aditya also glimpsed a beacon of hope—a glimmer of light shining through the darkness, guiding him towards his true purpose. For he saw that the artifact was not merely a tool of power—it was a catalyst for transformation, a force for good in a world consumed by darkness.

With this newfound understanding, Aditya knew that his journey was far from over. The artifact held the key to unlocking untold power and wisdom, and he was determined to wield it wisely and responsibly, to ensure that the mistakes of the past were not repeated.

And so, with a sense of purpose burning in his heart, Aditya set out to continue his journey, armed with the knowledge that the true adventure lay not in the destination, but in the journey itself. For he knew that as long as there were mysteries left to uncover and challenges left to overcome, the flame of adventure would never be extinguished, and the forces of darkness would never prevail.

And as he stepped out of the ancient temple and into the light of a new day, Aditya knew that the future held endless possibilities, and that whatever challenges lay ahead, he would face them with courage and determination, secure in the knowledge that he had the power to shape his own destiny.

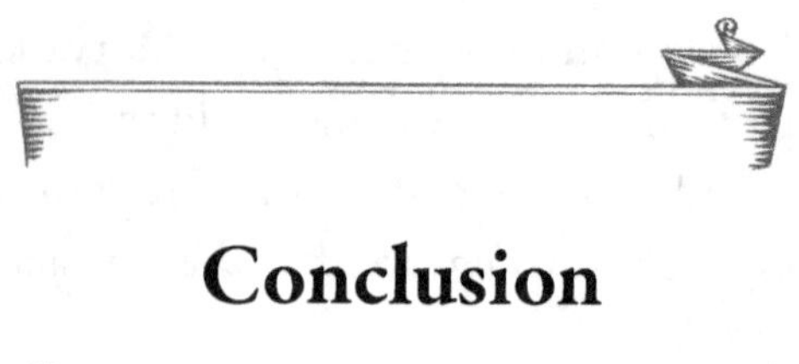

Conclusion

As the final chapter of Aditya's journey draws to a close, we find our hero standing on the precipice of a new dawn, his heart filled with the wisdom of ages past and the promise of a brighter future. Throughout his epic quest, Aditya has faced trials and tribulations beyond imagination, confronting ancient evils and unlocking mysteries that had long been shrouded in darkness.

But amidst the chaos and turmoil, Aditya has also discovered the true power that lies within—the power of courage, compassion, and resilience in the face of adversity. He has learned that true greatness is not measured by the battles we win or the enemies we vanquish, but by the strength of our convictions and the purity of our hearts.

As Aditya gazes out at the world stretched out before him, he knows that the journey is far from over. The forces of darkness may have been defeated, but new challenges await on the horizon, each more formidable than the last. But with his newfound allies and the wisdom of the ancients at his side, Aditya is ready to face whatever trials and tribulations lie ahead, secure in the knowledge that he has the power to shape his own destiny.

And so, as the sun sets on one chapter of his life and rises on the next, Aditya embraces the future with open arms, knowing that whatever adventures await, he will face them with courage and determination, secure in the knowledge that he is the master of his fate and the captain of his soul.

For in the end, it is not the destination that defines us, but the journey itself—the trials we face, the friends we make, and the lessons we learn along the way. And as Aditya sets out on his next great adventure, he knows that the greatest journey of all is the journey of the heart, where dreams become reality and destinies are forged in the fires of adversity.

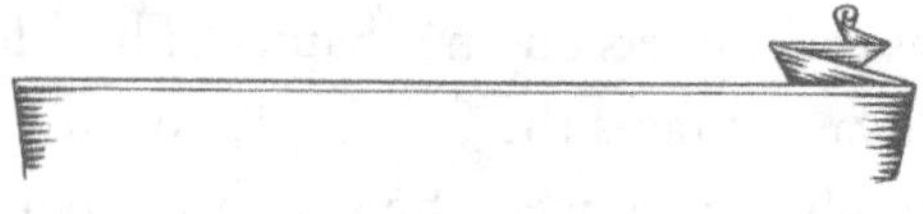

Thank You

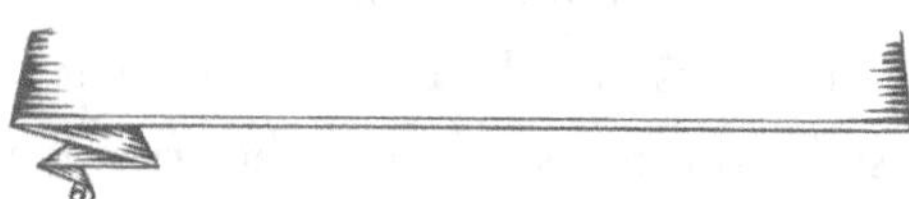

To all the readers who have embarked on this journey with Aditya, I extend my deepest gratitude. Your support and enthusiasm have been the driving force behind this tale, and I am truly grateful for the opportunity to share it with you.

A special thank you to those who have provided feedback, encouragement, and inspiration along the way. Your words have fueled my creativity and spurred me on to greater heights.

To the unsung heroes behind the scenes—the editors, publishers, and designers—who have worked tirelessly to bring this book to life, thank you for your dedication and passion.

Last but not least, to the characters who have leapt from the pages and into our hearts, thank you for sharing your stories with us. May your adventures live on in the imaginations of readers for years to come.

With heartfelt thanks,
Mrigendra Bharti

About the Author

Mrigendra Bharti, born on June 29, 2004, in South Delhi, India, is a multifaceted individual recognized as the owner of Mrigendra Bharti Group InfoTech India Co. Pvt Ltd. Beyond his entrepreneurial endeavors, he is a distinguished music producer, director, and a budding writer.

Embarking on his professional journey at a young age, Mrigendra Bharti's visionary leadership has led to the establishment of several successful ventures, including Croma Music Series Entertainment, Sellbrochure, Fauget Innovative, and more.

What sets Mrigendra apart is his early initiation into the world of business. His foray into the unknown realms of entrepreneurship began during his 10th-grade years, where he delved into the music industry. This initial venture laid the foundation for subsequent achievements, showcasing his dedication and resilience.

Having honed his skills in music, Mrigendra Bharti not only demonstrated significant growth in his craft but also expanded his professional network. His passion extends beyond music, encompassing app and website development, as well as graphic design.

Fueled by his creative aspirations, Mrigendra established the Mrigendra Bharti Group, a company specializing in website and app development. Currently, he collaborates with a dedicated team, collectively working on ambitious projects that promise innovation and excellence.

Mrigendra's journey serves as an inspiration, particularly for today's students, highlighting the potential of youthful determination and the ability to transform innovative ideas into successful businesses. As he continues to make strides in various domains, Mrigendra Bharti remains a dynamic force, contributing vibrancy to the realms of business, music, and technology.

Read more at https://www.imwriter-mrigendra.rf.gd.